Dear Parent:
Your child's love of readin

Every child learns to read in a different way and at his or her own speed. Some go back and forth between reading levels and read favorite books again and again. Others read through each level in order. You can help your young reader improve and become more confident by encouraging his or her own interests and abilities. From books your child reads with you to the first books he or she reads alone, there are I Can Read Books for every stage of reading:

SHARED READING
Basic language, word repetition, and whimsical illustrations, ideal for sharing with your emergent reader

BEGINNING READING
Short sentences, familiar words, and simple concepts for children eager to read on their own

READING WITH HELP
Engaging stories, longer sentences, and language play for developing readers

READING ALONE
Complex plots, challenging vocabulary, and high-interest topics for the independent reader

ADVANCED READING
Short paragraphs, chapters, and exciting themes for the perfect bridge to chapter books

I Can Read Books have introduced children to the joy of reading since 1957. Featuring award-winning authors and illustrators and a fabulous cast of beloved characters, I Can Read Books set the standard for beginning readers.

A lifetime of discovery begins with the magical words **"I Can Read!"**

Visit www.icanread.com for information
on enriching your child's reading experience.

For my sisters, Mary and Fredda
—H. P.

For Kevin and Ian
—L. S.

Watercolor and black pen were used to prepare the full-color art.

I Can Read Book® is a trademark of HarperCollins Publishers.

Library of Congress Cataloging-in-Publication Data
Parish, Herman.
Amelia Bedelia talks turkey / by Herman Parish ; illustrations by Lynn Sweat.
p. cm. — (An I can read book)
"Greenwillow Books."
Summary: When Amelia Bedelia volunteers to fill in as director of a third-grade Thanksgiving play, she misunderstands everything from one girl's desire to play a big role to an opening night wish that she "break a leg," but all is well in the end.
ISBN 978-0-06-084352-6 (trade bdg.) — ISBN 978-0-06-084353-3 (lib. bdg.)
ISBN 978-0-06-084354-0 (pbk.)
[1. Theater—Fiction. 2. Schools—Fiction. 3. Thanksgiving Day—Fiction. 4. Household employees—Fiction.
5. Humorous stories.] I. Sweat, Lynn, ill. II. Title.
PZ7.P2185Arc 2008   [E]—dc22   2007048407

15 16 17 18 SCP 10 9 8 7

Amelia Bedelia
Talks Turkey

story by Herman Parish
pictures by Lynn Sweat

Greenwillow Books
An Imprint of HarperCollinsPublishers

It was a cool, crisp morning in November.

Amelia Bedelia and Cousin Alcolu

brought a visitor to school.

"May I help you?" asked a woman.

"I hope so," said Amelia Bedelia.

"The principal, Mrs. Bloom,

wants a pumpkin

for your Thanksgiving pageant."

"Are you Amelia Bedelia?" said the woman.

"That's me," said Amelia Bedelia.

"And this is Cousin Alcolu."

"Hello there," said the woman.

"Mrs. Bloom asked me to meet you.

I am Mrs. Carson, the acting principal."

"You convinced me," said Amelia Bedelia.

"Will you play a principal in the pageant?"

"I am not playing a part," said Mrs. Carson.

"I am the principal until Mrs. Bloom returns."

"Where did she go?" asked Cousin Alcolu.

"Flu," said Mrs. Carson.

"Flew?" said Amelia Bedelia.

"Where did she fly?"

"She did not catch a plane," said Mrs. Carson.

"She caught a virus.

Every third-grade teacher is out sick."

"That's awful," said Cousin Alcolu.

"It gets worse," said Mrs. Carson.

"The third graders are supposed to put on

the Thanksgiving pageant in a few days.

I'm afraid we'll have to cancel it."

"I'd be happy to help them,"

said Amelia Bedelia.

"You would? What a relief!" said Mrs. Carson.

"Can I help out, too?" said Cousin Alcolu.

"I'm real handy at building things."

"This is wonderful," said Mrs. Carson.

"Let's go to the auditorium.

I will introduce you to the children."

On the way, Mrs. Carson

showed off the artwork.

"A few students are absent," Mrs. Carson said.

"Others are new or need parts.

You'll have to juggle them around."

The stage was filled with third graders.

"Attention everyone," said Mrs. Carson.

"Gather around and meet Amelia Bedelia.

She is here to help you rehearse your play.

Listen to her and do exactly what she says."

The kids stared at Amelia Bedelia.

"You all look nice," said Amelia Bedelia.

"But why are you wearing costumes now?

The pageant is a couple of days away."

"This is a dress rehearsal," said a boy.

"Is that so," said Amelia Bedelia.

"Then why aren't you wearing a dress?"

Everyone giggled.

11

"Because I play Myles Standish," said the boy.

"But you look more like a Pilgrim than I do."

"Thank you for saying that,"

said Amelia Bedelia.

"You make me feel right at home."

"There is one difference," said a girl.

"Your shoes don't have buckles."

She knelt down and put a pair of buckles

on Amelia Bedelia's shoes.

"How pretty," said Amelia Bedelia.

"They remind me of a nursery rhyme.

It goes 'One, two, buckle my shoe.'

Now I finally understand it."

"We should practice our lines,"

said the girl.

"Good idea," said Amelia Bedelia.

"Who wants to go first?"

"I should," said a boy.

"I am the narrator."

He turned toward the empty seats

and began to read.

13

"Wait a minute," said Amelia Bedelia.

"While you talk, the rest of the children

can practice their lines. Line up, everybody."

In no time at all, Amelia Bedelia

had lined up all of the third graders.

There was a line of boy Pilgrims,

a line of girl Pilgrims,

a line of boy Indians,

and a line of girl Indians.

"You sure know your lines!"

said Amelia Bedelia.

A boy walked up and said,

"May I have a different part?"

Amelia Bedelia looked at his hair.

"You sure can," she said.

She took a hairbrush out of her purse.

She parted his hair down the middle.

"That's a much better part,"

said Amelia Bedelia.

"I need an important part," said a girl.

"My mom told me to play a big role."

Amelia Bedelia thought a moment and said,

"There were lots of hungry

Pilgrims and Indians.

Tell your mom

that you'll play a very big roll.

I will make you a special costume."

"Thanks," said the girl. "She will be happy."

"I was not given anything to do," said a boy.

"Any suggestions?" asked Amelia Bedelia.

"My dad says I'm a big ham," he said.

"That's too bad," said Amelia Bedelia.

"Thanksgiving is for turkeys, not hams.

You could star in the Easter pageant."

"Easter is months away!" said the boy.

"You've got a point," said Amelia Bedelia.

"Let's add a ham to our Thanksgiving menu.

I will make you a special costume, too."

Amelia Bedelia looked

at everyone's costumes.

Something was missing.

"Ah-ha!" she said.

"Who is going to be the turkey?

Raise your wing

so I can see you."

"Tom was our turkey,"

said a girl.

"But he got sick and went home."

"Flu?" asked Cousin Alcolu.

"No," said the girl. "He walked."

"Yeah," said a boy. "Turkeys can't fly.

That's why they wind up on the table."

"Wild turkeys can fly," said a tall girl.

"They are also very smart birds."

"Who are you?" asked Amelia Bedelia.

"My name is Diana," said the girl.

"That's the new kid," said a boy.

"She's the biggest turkey I ever saw."

A couple of kids laughed.

Amelia Bedelia ignored them.

"Well, Diana," said Amelia Bedelia,

"since you know so much about turkeys,

how would you like to be one?

I'll make you an extra-special costume."

The kids who had laughed

weren't laughing now.

"Great!" said Diana. "I'll be your turkey."

Amelia Bedelia measured Diana

for her costume.

"After you get dressed," she said,

"you'll need some stuffing."

"Every turkey does," said Diana.

"Say, do you know the difference

between stuffing and dressing?"

"I'm not sure," said Amelia Bedelia.

"There is a dressing room over there.

I wonder where the stuffing room is?"

One of the Pilgrim girls spoke up.

"Stuffing is the stuff you stuff

inside the turkey.

Dressing is just extra stuffing

that couldn't be stuffed in."

"Why, thank you!" said Amelia Bedelia.

"All I know is that after Thanksgiving,

I am the one who feels stuffed."

"Me too," said Diana.

23

"Hey, Cousin Alcolu," said Amelia Bedelia.

"Can you build an oven to roast the turkey?"

"That's not how the Pilgrims cooked," said a girl.

"Their turkey was spit-roasted."

"Yuck!" said Amelia Bedelia.

"Who wants to eat a turkey roasted in spit?"

A boy laughed, and then he explained.

"They didn't cook the turkey in spit.

They cooked the turkey on a spit."

He showed them a picture in a history book.

Another boy wheeled out a cart.

"Gangway!" he said.

"When they talk about the harvest,

I'll come out to show our crops."

"Good work," said Cousin Alcolu.

"Can you manage that huge pumpkin?"

"I think so," said the boy.

"Pumpkins are just a big type of squash."

"Be careful," said Amelia Bedelia.

"That pumpkin weighs more than you do.
I'd hate for it to squash you."

"I almost forgot," said a girl.

"We need to make sweet potatoes, too."

"Potatoes aren't sweet," said Amelia Bedelia.

"They can be," said a boy.

"My grandma makes them taste like candy."

"I know what I'll do," said Amelia Bedelia.

"I'll make a batch of french fries

and sprinkle them with sugar."

"Sounds yummy," said Cousin Alcolu.

For the next few days,

Amelia Bedelia solved problems,

big and small.

Cousin Alcolu built props

just the way she told him to.

Finally, it was the day of the pageant.

The auditorium was filled with families,

friends, teachers, and other students.

Best of all, the third-grade teachers

and principal felt well enough to come.

Mr. and Mrs. Rogers showed up

to see if Amelia Bedelia needed help.

"Pardon me," said Mr. Rogers.

"You look like someone

who used to work at my house."

"I still do," said Amelia Bedelia.

"Don't I?"

"He's just teasing," said Mrs. Rogers.

"I deserve it," said Amelia Bedelia.

"I've spent so much time with the kids.

Thank you for coming to see the pageant."

The two principals joined them.

"Amelia Bedelia is amazing," said Mrs. Carson.

"I didn't have to worry about the pageant at all."

"Hope you like our changes,"

said Amelia Bedelia.

"Changes?" asked Mrs. Bloom. "What changes?"

"Some improvements," said Amelia Bedelia.

"We brought the Thanksgiving story up to date."

Now both principals looked very worried.

"Please excuse me," said Amelia Bedelia.

"Cousin Alcolu and I are the only stagehands.

We have to get everything ready."

"Good luck," said Mrs. Rogers.

"Break a leg!" said Mr. Rogers.

Amelia Bedelia stopped in her tracks.

"You must really be mad at me,

if you want me to break my leg," she said.

"Of course not," said Mr. Rogers.

"That is a tradition in the theater.

Saying 'Break a leg' means 'good luck.'"

"That is wacky," said Amelia Bedelia.

"'Break a leg' sounds like good luck

for the emergency room."

Backstage, the third graders were nervous.

"Everybody relax," said Amelia Bedelia.

"You've rehearsed. You know what to do.

Go out there and have some fun."

"We'll have fun afterward," said a girl.

"The parents are giving us a cast party."

"A cast party?" said Amelia Bedelia.

"That reminds me—nobody break a leg."

The children took their places.

The lights went down.

The curtain went up.

The audience applauded politely.

The narrator walked out and began,

"In the year 1620, the *Mayflower*

sailed from Europe to the New World."

The Pilgrims sang out:

"One, two, buckle my shoe.

Three, four, head for the shore."

The ship ran into Plymouth Rock.

"Here we are," said Myles Standish.

"This is the right address.

1620 Plymouth Rock.

Follow me!"

When he jumped onto Plymouth Rock,

the whole thing collapsed.

"Hey!" said a girl.

"You're supposed to land

on Plymouth Rock, not flatten it!"

In the audience, Mr. Rogers began to laugh.

An elbow from Mrs. Rogers

cured him of that.

The narrator continued,

"The Pilgrims suffered many hardships.

The winter was bitterly cold."

Cousin Alcolu stood on a ladder.

To represent winter, he dangled

a large snowflake he had built.

"The snow was deep,"

said the narrator.

"Big flakes fell on Plymouth Colony."

Just then, Cousin Alcolu lost his grip.

The snowflake hit the stage and rolled away.

"That was so cool!" yelled a fourth grader.

"Yeah," shouted another.

"The snow really fell!"

Even some parents applauded.

The narrator continued,

"When spring came,

the Pilgrims planted corn

and other crops

with the help

of their Indian friend Squanto.

He showed the Pilgrims a neat trick.

If you plant corn with some fish,

it will fertilize the seed

and grow better corn."

A chorus of Pilgrims chanted,

"Five, six, plant with fish sticks."

As the Pilgrims put in the fish sticks,

Squanto explained to the audience,

"You're supposed to use a real fish,

but that would stink up

the whole school."

As the Pilgrims watered the corn,

Amelia Bedelia slowly pulled on a string.

Corn appeared to grow up to the sky.

In the audience, a child yelled out,

"Look—those fish sticks really work!"

The narrator continued,

"The Pilgrims took good care of their crops.

Squanto taught them how to fish and hunt."

"Working together," said the narrator,

"they gathered enough

meat and fish

to last through

the coming winter."

Backstage,

Amelia Bedelia stood on a ladder.

She flung colored leaves

to show it was fall.

Suddenly, she lost her balance.

The ladder tipped over and . . .

SQUONCH!

Luckily, the pumpkin broke her fall.

"Uh-oh!" said Amelia Bedelia.

"I squashed Cousin Alcolu's squash."

The boy in charge of the cart

did not notice Amelia Bedelia.

He wheeled it out onstage.

The narrator continued,

"When autumn arrived,

the Pilgrims harvested

corn, beans, and squash.

They also gathered nuts."

Mr. Rogers saw Amelia Bedelia

being pulled out of the pumpkin.

He said to Mrs. Rogers,

"That is one big nut, all right.

I hope she didn't

break her leg."

They were relieved

to see Amelia Bedelia

tiptoe offstage.

"In fact," said the narrator,

"the Pilgrims had so much food

that they decided to have a feast

to celebrate and give thanks."

As they pretended to cook,

a chorus of Pilgrim girls sang.

"Seven, eight, set out the plates.

Nine, ten, invite our Indian friends."

"They cooked and cooked,"

said the narrator,

"and never used a microwave."

The audience clapped.

"Since that first Thanksgiving

lasted for three days,

there weren't any leftovers."

The audience clapped louder.

"Pilgrims and Indians

competed in games.

But, win or lose,

they were all good sports."

The audience cheered.

"There was plenty of food,"

said the narrator.

A Large Roll stepped out onstage.

A Big Ham joined her.

They both got plenty of applause.

Their parents were very proud.

"Of course," said the narrator,

"there was a ton of turkey."

When Diana made her entrance,

the audience went wild.

"Uh-oh," said Amelia Bedelia to herself.

"Diana looks pretty nervous.

I'll bet she forgot what to say."

Amelia Bedelia called out

from backstage.

"Pssst, Diana," she whispered loudly.

"You're suppose to say

'Gobble gobble!'

Say 'Gobble gobble!'"

All the other kids heard Amelia Bedelia.

They thought she was talking to them.

They did exactly what she told them to do.

The whole audience joined in.

It sounded like a flock of turkeys

had been let loose in the school.

Two children carried out a giant wishbone.

As they snapped it,

the entire cast hollered,

"We wish you a Happy Thanksgiving!"

As Diana turned around to watch,

she lost her balance

and fell off the stage.

She fell right into the arms of Mrs. Carson.

The audience thought it was part of the play.

They stood up and clapped loudly.

BRAVO! HOORAY! YAY!

The cast party was great fun.

Amelia Bedelia's sweet potatoes

were a hit.

So was Diana.

All the kids surrounded her.

The boy who had called her a turkey said,

"Diana, you deserve a new nickname.

We'd like to call you Wings,

because you winged it

and flew off the stage.

What do you say?"

Diana nodded, smiled, and said,

"Gobble gobble!"

Mrs. Bloom and Mrs. Carson

joined the party.

"Hi, Mrs. Carson," said Amelia Bedelia.

"Thank you for acting in the pageant."

"I made a lucky catch," said Mrs. Carson.

"Sometimes an acting principal

has to act fast."

"I'm glad you did," said Diana.

"I almost got the stuffing

knocked out of me."

"Amelia Bedelia," said Mrs. Bloom,

"this Thanksgiving,

I am thankful for you

and Cousin Alcolu."

"I am thankful, too," said Amelia Bedelia.

"I am thankful

that no one broke a leg."

"Or a drumstick," said Cousin Alcolu.

"Well done," said Mr. Rogers.

"I am thankful for both of you.

This is the first Thanksgiving pageant

I've been to that wasn't a turkey."

Mrs. Rogers noticed

that the pumpkin's blue ribbon

was stuck on Amelia Bedelia.

She plucked it off and put it on Diana.

"Congratulations," she said.

"You're a prize-winning pair."

On their way home, Mr. Rogers said,

"Thanksgiving is my favorite holiday.

I look forward to carving the turkey."

Amelia Bedelia was very impressed.

She had no idea he was a sculptor.

61

"I love Thanksgiving, too,"

said Mrs. Rogers.

"No presents to buy, wrap, or return."

"That's true," said Amelia Bedelia.

"It's all about family and food.

I've got a new recipe

for sweet potatoes."

"I can't wait to try it," said Mr. Rogers.

"You're a Thanksgiving expert by now."

"Not yet," said Amelia Bedelia.

"There is one thing I was wondering.

When you count your blessings,

and you run out of fingers,

is it okay to use your toes?"

Mr. and Mrs. Rogers looked at each other.

Neither of them spoke for a while.

Then Mrs. Rogers said, "Yes, of course."

Mr. Rogers added, "That's what we do."

He pulled into their driveway.

"Home, sweet home," said Amelia Bedelia.